I Miss You, Stinky Face

Written by:
Lisa McCourt

Illustrated by:
Cyd Moore

HINKLER BOOKS

For Tucker...LM. ☺ ☺ ☺ For Ran and Jay...CM.

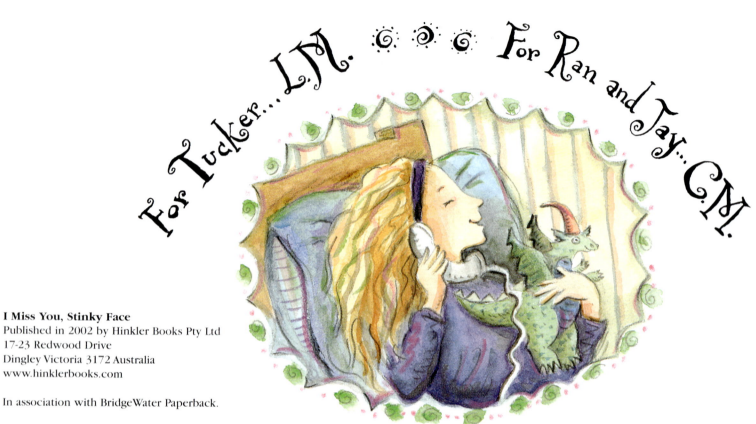

I Miss You, Stinky Face
Published in 2002 by Hinkler Books Pty Ltd
17-23 Redwood Drive
Dingley Victoria 3172 Australia
www.hinklerbooks.com

In association with BridgeWater Paperback.

Previously published by BridgeWater Paperback, an imprint and
trademark of Troll Communications L.L.C. in 2000.

Text copyright © Lisa McCourt 1999.
Illustrations copyright © Cyd Moore 1999.

1 86515 744 9

Printed and bound in China.

"I miss you, my little Stinky Face," said Mama on the phone.
But I had a question.

Mama, do you miss me so much that you're coming right home to me, no matter what?

"I'm coming today," said Mama, "on a big silver airplane."

But, Mama, but, Mama, what if the airplane forgets how to fly?

"If that airplane forgets how to fly, I'll hop in the basket of a hot-air balloon. I'll soar past clouds and stars until I see your window, then I'll float right into your room."

But, Mama, what if the balloon runs out of hot air and you have to land in the middle of the desert?

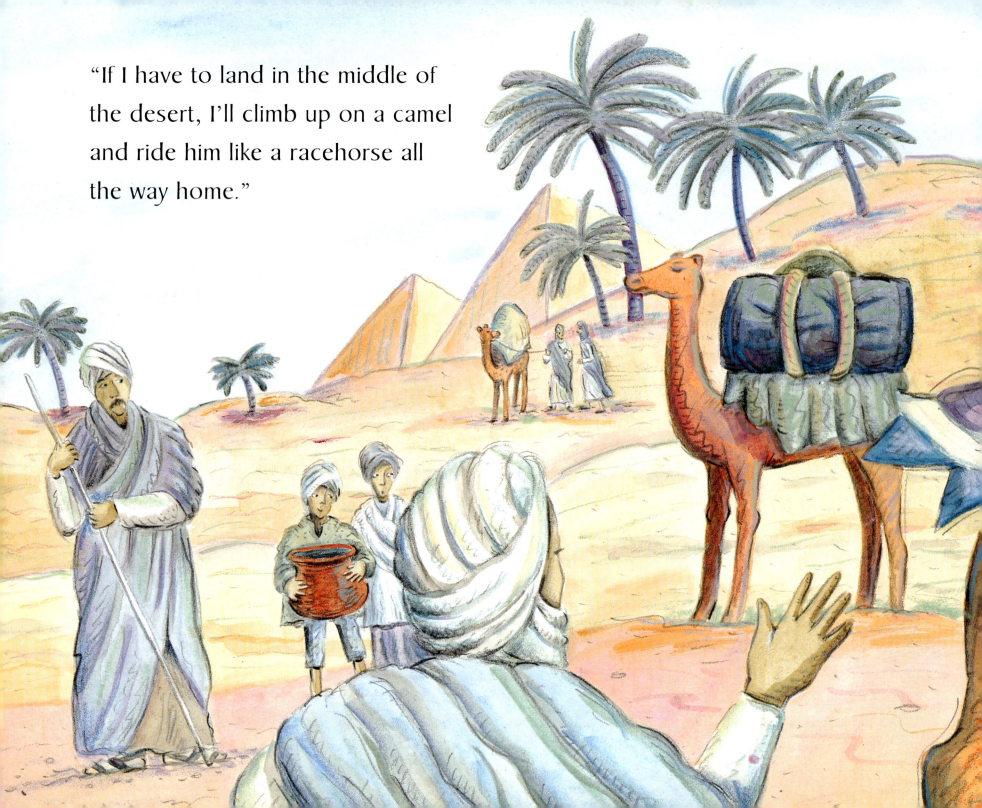

"If I have to land in the middle of the desert, I'll climb up on a camel and ride him like a racehorse all the way home."

But, Mama, but, Mama, what if the camel gets so tired that he just won't take another step and he leaves you stranded in the jungle?

"Then I'll search that jungle for a cheetah, the fastest animal there is. I'll jump on her back, and she'll race me straight home to you."

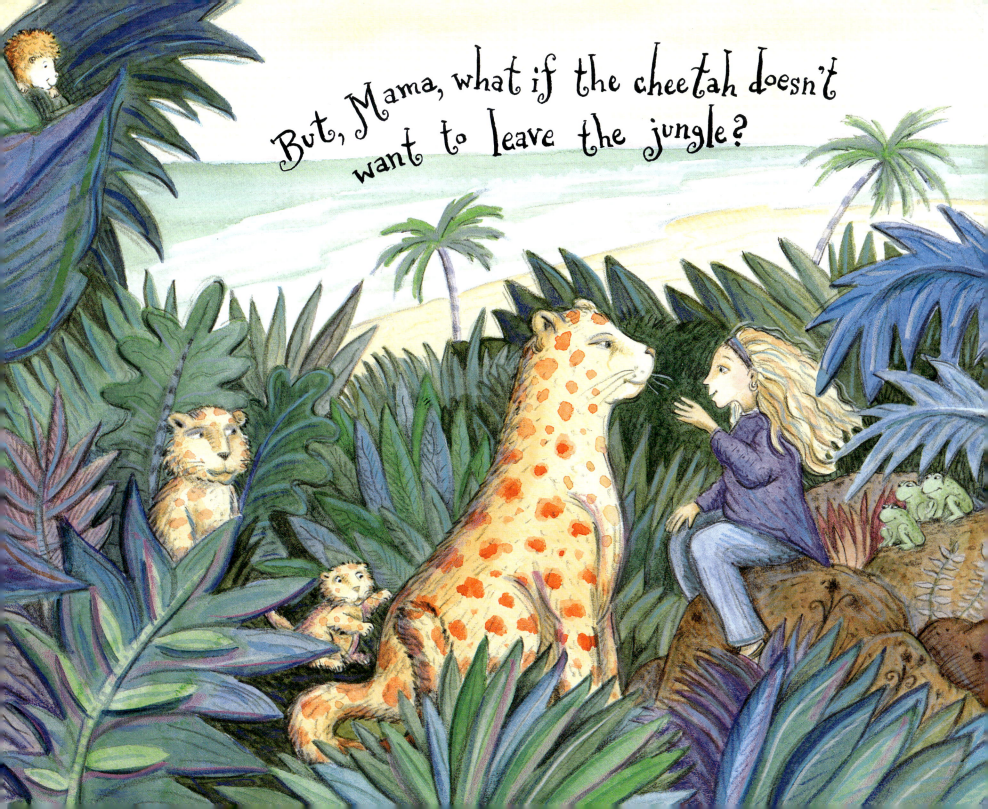

But, Mama, what if the cheetah doesn't want to leave the jungle?

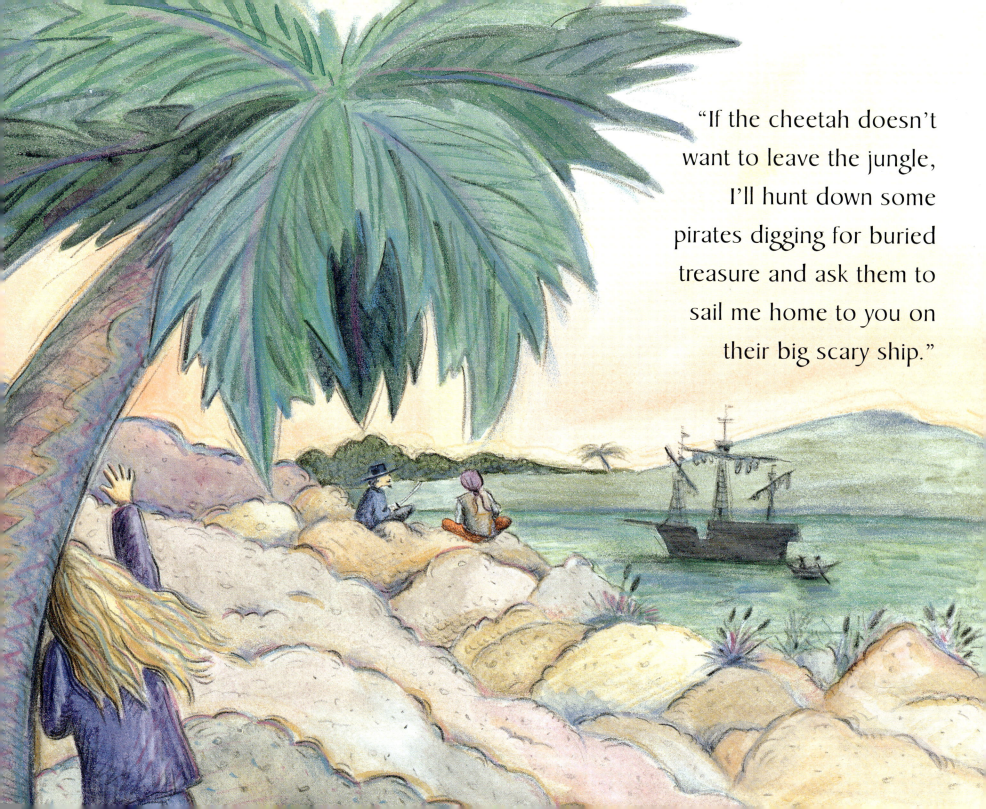

"If the cheetah doesn't want to leave the jungle, I'll hunt down some pirates digging for buried treasure and ask them to sail me home to you on their big scary ship."

But, Mama, what if the terrible pirates make you walk the gangplank?

"Then I'll find the speediest shark in the ocean. I'll grab on to his fin and use it to steer, and we'll skim through the high seas all the way home to you."

But, Mama, what if the shark wants to nibble you into a million tiny pieces?

"If the shark tries that, I'll leap from his greedy jaws and body surf to shore. I'll call the bravest astronauts and hitch a ride on their supersonic spaceship, and we'll all be home to you faster than the speed of light."

But, Mama, what if their spaceship gets sucked through a black hole and takes you far back in time to a big old castle instead of to our house?

"If the spaceship lands that far back in time, I'll look around for a magic dragon.

"I'll climb way up on her back
and whisper in her ear just
how much I miss you.
The magic dragon will fly me
through time right back to you."

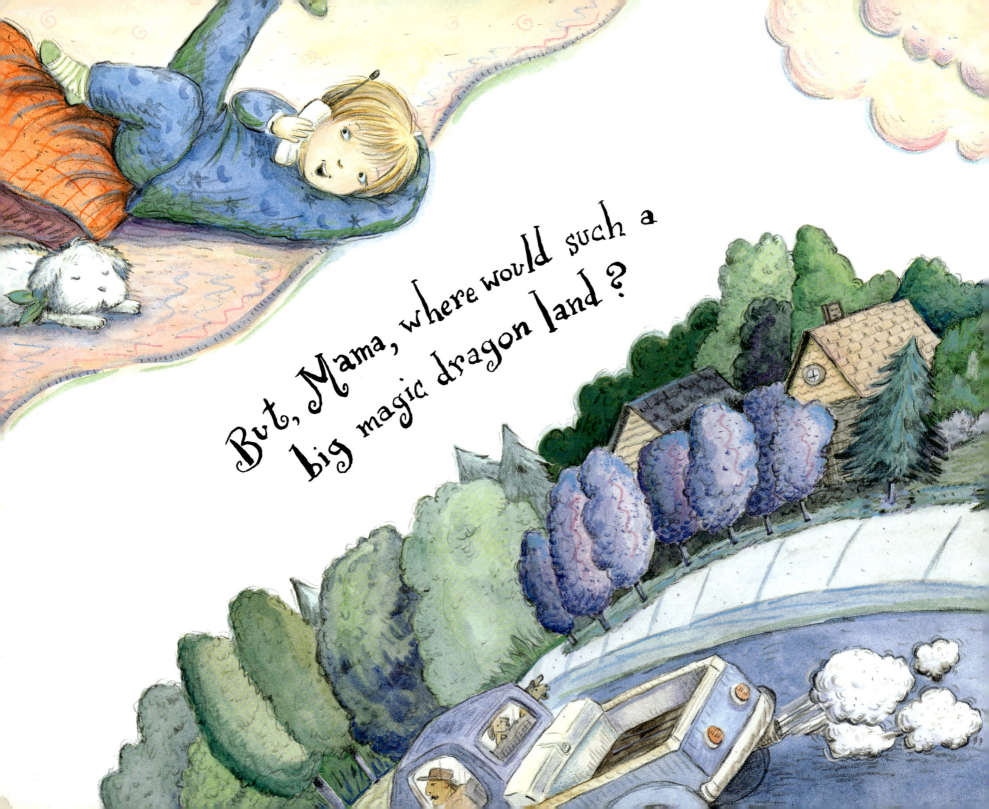

But, Mama, where would such a big magic dragon land?

"I think there's enough room on the driveway if you make sure your bike's put away."

I'll put it away.... But, Mama, the airplane is how you'll probably come home, right?

"Probably."

I miss you, Mama.

"And I miss you, my little Stinky Face."